THE Ear

Thames & Hudson

THE Ear

PIRET RAUD

When the Ear woke up one morning,
she discovered that she was all alone.

Where was the head on whom
the Ear had lived her whole life?

She looked around, but the head had left.

The Ear was headless, without the head.

What use was she to anyone like that?

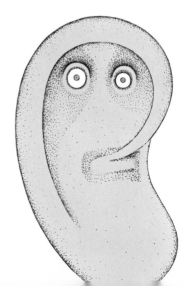

The world is a big place.

Where should she go?

What should she do?

How should she carry on?

The Ear was confused.

She didn't know who she was anymore.

"The head always knew what to do,
because the head was the brains.
But without a head, I am no one," sobbed the Ear.

Suddenly, she heard someone say "Croak!"

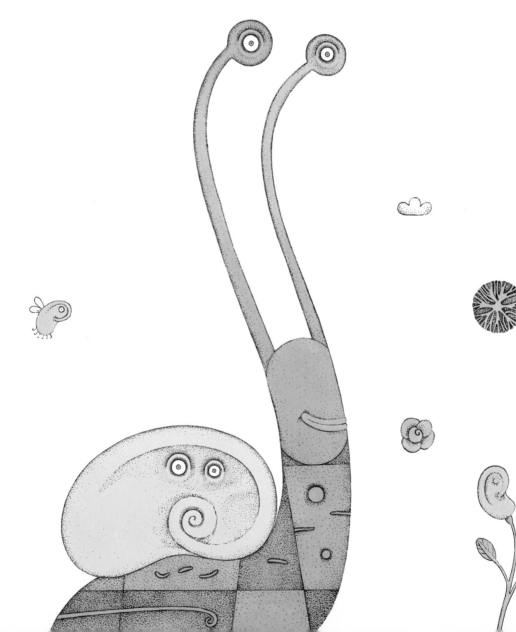

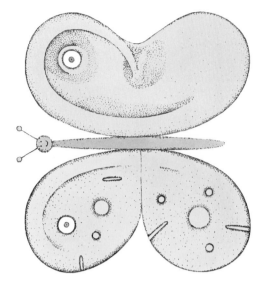

It was a frog.

"Dear Ear," asked the frog.

"Could you perhaps listen to me sing?

My heart is heavy and when I sing I feel lighter.

My voice is terribly croaky, but I still long

to sing for someone."

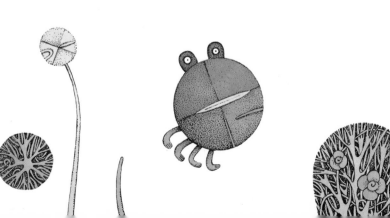

The Ear kindly agreed.

She didn't need the head
to listen to the frog's song.
The frog felt better for singing
and the Ear felt a little happier too.

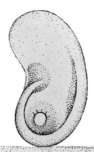

The next day an elephant came to see the Ear.

"They say you are a good listener," said the elephant.
"I feel terribly sad. If you could listen to my worries,
my heart might feel lighter."

The Ear gladly agreed. The elephant told a story
about how a twist of fate had brought him across
the sea and far from home.

"My home is in a faraway land. I miss my grandmother.
I miss the stars in the southern sky, the baobabs
and the blue daisies."

The Ear was sorry for the elephant,
but the elephant felt brighter.

When the elephant had left, a hare showed up to meet the Ear.

"Dear Ear, I must confess! I have done something bad
and it worries me. If I could tell you about my mischief,
my heart might feel lighter."

The hare told the Ear how she had eaten a snowman's nose.

"The snowman melted long ago, but it still bothers me.
I will never eat someone's nose again."

The Ear understood her, and the hare stopped worrying.

Before long, the Ear was famous for being the best listener in the land. Creatures came from far and wide hoping for a chance to be heard.

The Ear listened to everyone's problems, and everyone felt better.
The Ear was pleased that she could help them all, just by listening!

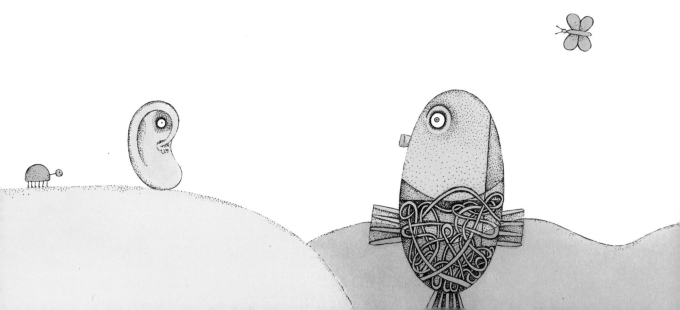

But one day an evil spider appeared.

"My dear little Ear," said the spider, with a voice as sweet as honey.
"I like you the best, the others are so stupid. The frog can't
sing at all, he just croaks awfully, and the elephant has
an ugly trunk and should go back to where he came from.
And that hare is a nasty thief! Only you and I are cool!"

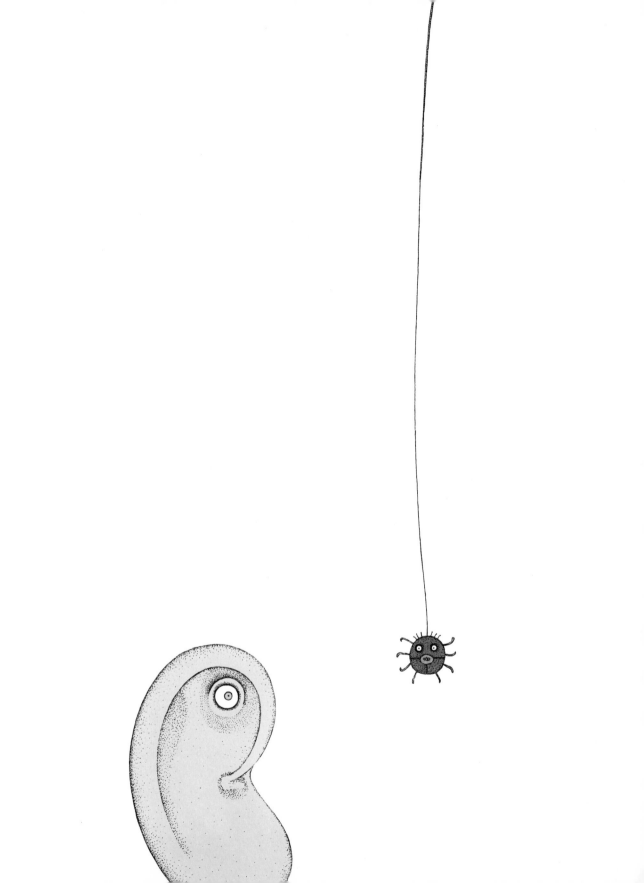

The Ear didn't like hearing the spider's poisonous words.
Listening made her ache.

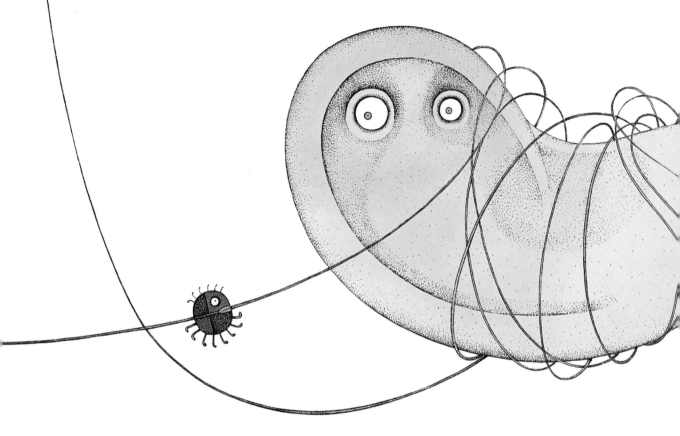

The spider had something bad to say about everyone.
She talked and talked, and all the while she wound her
evil thread around the Ear.

Now the Ear ached all over. She tried to wriggle free
but she was trapped.

"Oh, I wish the head was here!" she thought.
"He could shut that spider up!"

But there was no head.

Help came from somewhere the Ear didn't expect at all.

A big tongue came whizzing through the air.

"Chomp!" gulped the frog, and the spider was gone.

Then came the elephant and blew away the tangled thread with his trunk. The hare rushed up and hugged the Ear, stroking her gently so she stopped aching.

The Ear felt much better.

From that day on she never thought of the head again.
She was very happy among her new friends.

First published in 2018 in the United States of America by
Thames & Hudson Inc., 500 Fifth Avenue, New York, New York 10110

www.thamesandhudsonusa.com

Library of Congress Control Number: 2018945317

ISBN 978-0-500-65163-6

Printed and bound in China by Toppan Leefung Printing Limited